D0558827

Stinky Steve
Book 4

Minecraft Steve Meets
the Burpinator

Cover Design by John Over, 2017
ISBN: 978-1542877480
Copyright © 2017 by Montage Publishing
All rights reserved
www.montagepublishing.com

CHAPTER ONE

It's been a busy week on the server.

Unlike the other citizens of Minecraft, I don't

get to call it a day at 5pm and crack open a

frosty can of soda. Nope, being a superhero

is a 24/7 job.

But I don't mind the workload. To tell

you the truth, it's nice to be needed and the

citizens I save are always so thankful. It might

be hard to believe, but these unstoppable

farts may just be the best thing that's ever

happened to me. I just wish nice people

would hang out with me after I rescue them.

This week alone I saved a Steve who

got stuck in a tree. He climbed way up to the

top to rescue his pet ocelot. But the ocelot

jumped down, landing on its feet, leaving his

Steve high and dry. Luckily my farts were toxic

enough to decay the leaves and branches on

impact, allowing my new pal Steve to slide

down to safety.

I also saved a fair maiden's castle from

being destroyed by a landslide. I hung on to

the tallest turret and timed my butt blast

perfectly to re-route the course of the falling rocks and mud. She sure was thankful, but she said no when I asked her out on a date. I wasn't offended - girls aren't usually too keen on farts. But saving her castle was all in a day's work.

My biggest feat was helping an entire village escape from a roaming pack of wolves. I lured the wolves away from the villagers' homes with a couple of dead birds who had the bad luck of flying behind me. Then I flew in circles to corral the wolfs in a thick,

impenetrable force-field of farts (I call it the

Fartsfield – patent pending). Wolves have a

heightened sense of smell and this stink was

pretty intense, even for me. I can't imagine

how putrid it must have been for the wolves.

As cool as it is saving all these people, I'm always looking over my shoulder for the Burpinator. I know he's out there somewhere, one step ahead of me. If only I could figure out who he was, or what he wants... I'm a reasonable guy; I'm sure we could work something out. Just in case, I've been working on a new burp detector device. So far all it has detected are my farts. I'm still working out the kinks.

CHAPTER TWO

When the burp detector alarm stops

I hear a faint - but desperate - cry for help.

Someone's in trouble! It's time to suit up!

I pull on my iron leggings and strap on

my gas mask, but being a superhero isn't just

about what's on the outside. The real power

comes from the INSIDE, so I slurp down two

full bowls of beans.

Cramp. Gurgle. Lurch.

I zoom into the sky and try to hone in on the voice calling for help. It sounds like it's coming from the old amusement park. The place shut down long ago and is now a hotbed for creepers and zombies. Who in their right mind would go in there now? Sometimes I wonder if I'm saving people from danger or their own stupidity.

When I get closer to the amusement park, I see the place is chock full of zombies - just as I suspected. Time to get down to buttsness (it's like business, but with my butt).

I throw down a few fart bombs to shake out any hiding zombies and distract them away from whoever is trapped. I get them all good and mad then I land right in the middle of them.

I've got the zombies right where I want them! I reach into my backpack and take out some flint and steel. I strike them together and get enough of a spark to light my torch.

"I like my zombies the way I like my burgers," I say.

I bend down and put the torch right by

the seat of my pants.

"Well done."

ROAAARR!

I let out a steady, concentrated fart

that funnels the lit match and turns my rear

end into a flame thrower. Suddenly, I'm

roasting 360 degrees of zombie scum. "Help,

pleeeeease!" a non-zombie voice calls.

The call for help is coming from the Hall of Mirrors!

I run inside the hall but as soon as I'm in, WHAM, the doors shut behind me. Someone slides a shovel between the door handles and I can't get out. I'm trapped!

On the other side of the glass, the cries for help get closer and closer until I detect someone staring at me from the other side. It's Alex.

"Oh Steve, please help me! Help me!"

she says.

"I'd be happy to, if you can help me get

out of here first!"

I pound on my side of the glass but

there's no getting out.

Alex starts laughing. Louder and louder

until in the middle of laughing she lets out a

huge BURP.

"Excuse me," she says with an evil smile.

No – it can't be! The Burpinator is a girl?!

CHAPTER THREE

"So we finally meet," I say.

"I wish you could see the look on your face. Oh! You can, we're in the hall of mirrors. Just turn around." The Burpinator continues to laugh.

Like I'm gonna fall for that. Superhero rule #1: never turn your back on your nemesis.

Alex uses a voice that makes me think she's imitating someone - namely me.

"Hi. I'm Super Steve. I save everyone in Minecraft with my stink powers. I'm sooooo great." She switches back to her regular voice. "All you're doing is causing pollution!"

Speaking of pollution, the double dose of beans I scarfed down earlier isn't done with me yet. My stomach churns; soon I'll be leaking gas everywhere.

"There can only be ONE superhero in Minecraft, Steve. You're no match for The Burpinator. It's time for you to give up."

"Never!" I pound the glass with my fist, but it's no use. The brown cloud forming under me is already at knee level.

"Suit yourself," she says. "If you don't want to give up being a superhero voluntarily, I'll just watch you slowly destroy yourself with your own farts."

The stinky fog surrounding me steadily climbs higher and higher. My clean air supply is shrinking by the second. Why did I eat TWO bowls of beans?!

For the first time since I discovered my superpowers, I'm scared. Until I see what's approaching the Burpinator from behind.

Alex continues to watch me suffer but doesn't see the group of zombies walking towards her.

She's certainly made it clear we aren't friends, so I feel under no obligation to tell her she's about to be the main course at an all-you-can-eat zombie buffet.

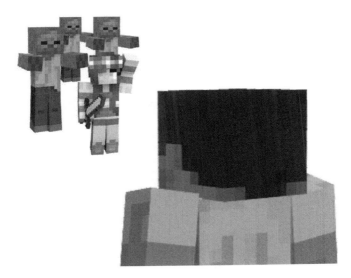

Unfortunately, The Burpinator is pretty smart. She catches my eyes looking over her shoulder and whips around to follow my gaze.

"Zombies again? Sit tight and watch how a REAL superhero handles this."

The Burpinator zooms over to the concession stand across from the Hall of Mirrors and hops over the counter, out of view. In just a few seconds, she leaps out again and lands before the army of zombies.

She opens her mouth and lets out the loudest supersonic burp I've ever heard.

I'd be impressed if, you know, she wasn't trying to end me.

She's doing a good job, too— my farts have me surrounded. I'm running out of oxygen and feeling nauseous and woozy. I drop to my knees and try to breathe through my shirt. It barely helps.

Everything is going dark and fuzzy, but I catch The Burpinator kicking zombie butt. Her super burps launch several zombies into the air. Just as I'm about to lose consciousness, she turns and faces another herd of zombies. This time, her monstrous belch picks up a trash can and a bench and sends them FLYING into the glass doors of the Hall of Mirrors.

They shatter upon impact and my noxious

gasses disperse into the atmosphere.

I take a HUGE breath of fresh, clean

air and climb to my feet. Time to escape! I

blast into the sky, putting as much distance

as possible between the Burpinator and me.

I hear her screams far below me.

CHAPTER FOUR

Think, Steve. This is no ordinary super

villain you're dealing with. No, this foe is extra

powerful... GIRL powerful. This isn't the kind

of battle I can win with my butt. With a girl,

you also have have to use your brain.

To beat an evil genius, you've got to think like an evil genius. The Burpinator probably expects me to flee far, far away after a such a rancid brush with death, so I decide to surprise her and head back to the abandoned amusement park.

If I were a supervillain, an abandoned amusement park would be the perfect home base. No one around to snoop into your evil plans - plus, all the soda, snacks, and free rides you can handle. Wait a minute... that sounds awesome! I hate to say it, but this girl really might be a genius. I duck into a minecart on

an out-of-commission rollercoaster.

From here I can see the whole park

beneath me without being seen. Okay... if I'd

just fought a platoon and a half of zombies

and accidently set my nemesis free after I

had him right where I wanted him, where would I go? I'd be exhausted - and mad - and I'd probably want to cool down with an ice cold....

BINGO!

I scan the park for the concession stand, and sure enough there's the Burpinator angrily stomping around behind the counter. I should be a detective. She comes out with the BIGGEST cup of soda I've ever seen, so huge she has to use two hands to hold it. I can

understand wanting to drown your sorrows,

but this is ridiculous.

She takes a drink and a few seconds

later, lets out a loud burp.

So that's how she's getting her

powers!

I watch the Burpinator take her giant

cup of burp juice onto the carousel.

She may be an evil belch-ridden

genius, but she's still a girl. She chooses the

unicorn with the pink mane.

Now's my chance. I hop down from

the minecart coaster and make a dash for

the concession stand. Where could that soda

machine be-OOOH! COTTON CANDY!

My biggest weakness... not really. I just love cotton candy.

But back to the task at hand. When I find the fountain I'm looking for, it's no ordinary soda fountain. This is a dastardly dispenser of carbonated concoctions! Each flavor features a different potion to enchant and weaponize the gas in the Burpinator's gullet. Radioactive Root beer, Lemon-lime Liquefier, Ginger Ale Grenades, and the one she must have used fighting those zombies earlier - Sonic Sarsaparilla.

These are some pretty powerful potions, but I feel there's still room for improvement. These flavors could really pack a punch if they were somehow rigged with TNT... and luckily I just happen to have some on me with the Burpinator's name all over it.

I take out my supply of TNT and rig the soda fountain with the explosives.

If she presses a single button on this fountain, the TNT will detonate. The next time she comes by to fill up, she'll blow up.

"STEVE!"

I almost jump out of my skin.

"STEVE! I KNOW YOU'RE HERE!"

How does she know?!

"I CAN SMELL YOU."

CHAPTER FIVE

The Burpinator's voice gets closer; I can hear her sniffing me out. I make it out of the concession stand just as the Burpinator barges in. Uh-oh, better pick up the pace. It's only a matter of time before-

The concession stand shoots up into

the sky and lands on top of the carousel. But

the Burpinator is still standing, armed with

another giant cup of soda.

"YOU'LL PAY FOR THIS, STEVE!" she

screams. She takes a sip and aims a burp

straight toward me. Thankfully I have just

enough gas left in my stank-tank to safely

fart my way above it. Her burp hits the Ferris

wheel behind me and knocks it over with a

blinding explosion.

At least now I know what she's packing in that cup: Ginger Ale Grenade. I'm gonna need a miracle - and some more beans - pronto.

There's a hot dog cart in this park somewhere. There has to be. I remember coming here and always getting a fresh hot dog after working up an appetite screaming my head off on the roller coaster. The vendor had to make mine fresh because I couldn't handle the chili that came on the regular hotdogs. That spicy bean mixture gave me the worst gas I've ever had, but right now my life depends on it.

I don't have time to stroll down memory lane -The Burpinator keeps launching her gullet-grenades in my direction, and I'm running out of things to hide behind. Around the corner from the demolished Hall of Mirrors, I spot the red and yellow flags I'm looking for. The hot dog cart is only a few yards away. I just need a diversion to give me enough time to scarf down some chili and let it work its magic.

The Burpinator is still sniffing me out. If only there's a way to throw her off my scent. I absentmindedly reach into my pocket and touch upon the perfect solution. AHA! My cotton candy! I take out the fluffy wad of soft, sugary goodness. Unfortunately this sweet treat will have to be sacrificed in the good name of gas. Cotton is excellent at holding odors. I crouch down behind a garbage can and desperately squeeze out one last fart out onto the cotton candy.

FFFFT

(Sorry cotton candy.)

I've created the perfect decoy! I throw

my scent-double into a bumper car and run

in the opposite direction toward the hot dog

cart. It works like a charm.

The Burpinator follows my sent into the bumper car arena and I have enough time to chow down on fart fuel.

I'm half way through a bucket of chili when a sharp pain wrenches through my stomach. The cramps bring me to my knees, and I've never been so grateful to be so uncomfortable.

Stinky Steve is back!

CHAPTER SIX

"Here I am! Come out and fight me!" I

call out from what's left of the Hall of Mirrors.

The Burpinator arrives sooner than I

expected. "With pleasure." She takes another

long draw on her soda then pauses, turns her

head, and blasts a burp at me. Little does she

know, I'm excellent at fire drills - I stop, drop,

and roll out of the burp's path. It hits one of

the mirrors and ricochets back to send her

flying into a wall of oversized stuffed animals.

She's not hurt, but her ego is. She tries

to get up.

"I wouldn't do that If I were you." I

hover above her thanks to fart propulsion.

She stands up anyway into a thick haze of chili dog fog.

She coughs and her eyes water. "I warned you!" I say.

She takes a drink.

That tell-tale slurp sound lets us both know she's empty. Now's my chance!

She seeths and makes a break for the
concession stand. I zoom over her and start
crop-dusting her path with farts; I certainly
don't want her to fill up again. I don't want
to know what Lemon-Lime Liquefier can do.

The smell coming from my butt is especially rank, but The Burpinator is one tough cookie. She folds her straw in half and sticks an end up each nostril to plug her nose as she sprints to her soda supply.

She slides under the fountain like she's stealing home plate and drinks straight from the nozzles, gulping down gallons of each enchanted soda. I rush to stop her but am halted in my tracks by another massive, bubbling cramp. I can't move as the gas inflates my belly like a balloon animal.

Meanwhile, The Burpinator is still pressing the tap on the soda fountain, but nothing comes out.

She drank ALL the soda. Alex gets to her feet, swollen to twice her size with bubbles and fizz. She laughs the kind of maniacal laugh I've only heard in movies.

But I still can't move. The pressure of the gas builds inside me and doesn't come out. I knew that hot dog chili was a gamble. I'm going to implode and The Burpinator will be victorious.

Uh-oh, nevermind.

The biggest, loudest tornado of a fart ROARS out of my rear with a force so strong I have to hold on to the railing to keep from being propelled into space.

The massive blast hits the amusement park like an earthquake, shaking all the remaining rides and buildings down to to piles of dust and "You must be this tall to ride" signs.

When the last of the gas blast has passed, I land on my feet and face The Burpinator. Her hair's been blown straight back. If she weren't my nemesis, I'd almost think she looked cute. (Don't tell her I said that.)

"Are your ears ringing? Because mine are."

"Is that all you've got!" she yells. "Say goodbye, Steve!"

She opens her mouth, but nothing happens. We're both surprised and it actually gets a little awkward standing there, looking at each other in silence.

A low rumbling starts, deep from within the Burpinator's belly. Suddenly, she inflates like a human hot air balloon until her toes can't reach the ground.

"Whoa, whoa whoaaa!"

She's a good two feet above the

ground and keeps swelling, larger and larger.

WHOA!

"Steve! You have to help me!"

If I hadn't seen her drink all that soda

with my own eyes, I might think this was

another trap. But this time, her pleas are

real. She may be my nemesis, but she's still a citizen of Minecraft.

"Okay, stay calm," I say. "I'm going to help you, but you aren't going to like it."

"What does that mean?!"

I take out the diamond sword from my big backpack. "I hope you brought a good book with you," I say.

"Why?" she asks.

"Because, you're about to take a long flight." I stick the sword into the Burpinator's belly and she takes off across the blue Minecraft sky. The carbonated power of several gallons of enchanted soda hurl The Burpinator high into the air. In a matter of seconds, she's nothing but a tiny, furious dot on the horizon.

"I'LL GET YOU FOR THIS, STINKY STEVE!

YOU HAVEN'T SEEN THE LAST OF ME!"

Sigh. Girls just can't seem to get away

from me fast enough.

EPILOGUE

Since The Burpinator went soaring over the server to her fizzy demise, things have been pretty quiet around here. Too quiet. Of course, I don't let that stop me from taking a load off for a while. Back at home, I pop a couple of chickens in my furnace. A savory scent fills the air and for once it's not coming from my butt. It's so warm and toasty with the aroma of roasted chicken, I wish I had someone to share it with. But company

is hard to come by when you're a superhero,

and even harder to come by when your

superpower is stinky farts.

Who could that be?!

When I open the door, I find not a

person, but a package.

It's from The Burpinator. A bowl of beans and a note that says, *"This isn't over."*

Sure it is, I think. Totally and completely. But when I go back in the house, my chicken is gone. So is my treasure chest with everything I own!

Time to heat up some beans!

Did you like the Book?
If so, be sure to leave a review on Amazon.
The more reviews I get, the more books I'll write.

Don't forget to tell a friend!

MEET PT EVANS AUTHOR OF STINKY STEVE!

"It's Pooptastic!"

"Hey there! PT Evans is the name, writing books is my game. I love Minecraft, Pokemon, pizza, emojis, cats, and fart jokes (who doesn't?). When I'm not writing books or doing school visits, I can be found training alligators and sumo wrestling. Follow my adventures on Youtube, Instagram, Twitter, and Facebook."

Twitter: @PTEvansAuthor
Instagram: @PTEvansAuthor
Facebook: facebook.com/PTEvansAuthor

Need Minecraft advice on dealing with Creepers? Zombies? Farts? Now you can Ask Stinky Steve!

The popular - and flatulent - Minecraft superhero finally answers readers' questions on every topic from inventory to best friends to cutting the cheese. Join Stinky Steve as he puts his Minecraft knowledge to good use solving players' perplexing issues with hilarious, gassy advice.

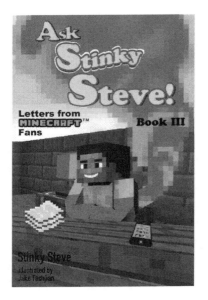

App Mash-up: Minecraft and Angry Birds

Jackson and Susie love to play games on their Mom's phone. But today, a freak power surge sends them INTO their favorite games. What a treat – to be INSIDE an app - until they find themselves under attack by creepers and zombies and some very irate birds. A must read for Minecraft and Angry Bird fans!

Minecat: A Feline Minecraft Adventure
Book One: A Whole Lot of Ocelots
Book Two: Sugar Cane Rush

Do you love to play Minecraft? Does your cat? Spike is an indoor cat who spawns into his owner's game. It doesn't take long before Spike goes from ocelot bait to King of the Jungle. Will he decide to stay in the wonderful world of Minecraft? Can he stay clear of the zombies and creepers? What would YOUR cat do???

Obsessed with Emojis?

LOL with your favorite emoji's as they come to life in this fun, new series. Follow Annie with the constant smile; Kevin, her devilish brother; Billy, poop head and BFF; and Dot, the love-struck jock as they make their way through Emoji Elementary.

Available at Amazon.com!

Twitter: @PTEvansAuthor
Instagram: @PTEvansAuthor
Facebook: facebook.com/PTEvansAuthor

MONTAGE PUBLISHING

Twitter: @MontageBooks
Instagram: @MontagePublishing
Facebook: facebook.com/montagepublishing
www.MontagePublishing.com

Thank you for Reading!

Made in the
USA
Middletown, DE